Series 606D

CINDERELLA

retold by
VERA SOUTHGATE, M.A., B.Com.

with illustrations by
ERIC WINTER

Publishers: Wills & Hepworth Ltd., Loughborough
First published 1964 *Printed in England*

CINDERELLA

Once upon a time there was a little girl called Cinderella. Her mother was dead, and she lived with her father and two elder sisters.

Cinderella's elder sisters were beautiful and fair of face but, because they were bad tempered and unkind, their faces grew to look ugly. They were jealous of Cinderella because she was a lovely child, and so they were often unkind to her.

The ugly sisters made Cinderella do all the work in the house. She carried coal for the fire, cooked the meals, washed the dishes, scrubbed and mended the clothes, swept the floor and dusted the furniture. She worked from morning till night, without stopping.

Cinderella not only did all the housework but she also helped her sisters to dress. She cleaned their shoes, brushed their hair, tied their ribbons and fastened their buckles. The elder sisters had many fine clothes, but they were so bad tempered that they still looked ugly.

Cinderella had no fine clothes. All she had was an old grey dress and a pair of wooden shoes.

In the evening, when she had worked until she was weary, Cinderella had no bed to go to. She had to sleep by the hearth in the cinders. That was why her sisters called her Cinderella and that was why she always looked dusty and dirty.

Now it happened that the King arranged a great feast for his son. The feast was to last three days and on each evening there was to be a grand ball. All the beautiful young girls in the country were invited, in order that the Prince might choose himself a bride.

Cinderella's sisters were invited to the feast and they were so excited that they could talk of nothing else. Cinderella was not invited. As she was only seen in rags, working in the kitchen, everyone thought that she was her sisters' maid.

On the evening of the first ball, Cinderella had to help her sisters to put on their new dresses and arrange their hair.

Cinderella thought of how she would like to have a ball-gown and go to the ball and see the prince. Tears began to run down her face.

"What are you crying for?" asked the ugly sisters, crossly.

"I would like to wear a beautiful dress and go to the ball," replied Cinderella.

"You, go to the ball!" laughed the sisters, "a fine sight you would be, at the ball!" And they pointed to her ragged dress and wooden shoes.

When her sisters had left for the ball, poor Cinderella sat down and cried as if her heart would break.

Suddenly Cinderella heard a kind voice saying, "What is the matter, my dear?" She jumped up from her stool and turned to see who it could be. There stood her fairy godmother, smiling kindly at her.

"I would like to have a beautiful dress and be able to go to the ball," said Cinderella. "I have never been to a ball and I have never had a ball-gown," she went on, "and I would love to see the prince."

"And so you shall, my dear," said her fairy godmother. "Dry your eyes and then do exactly as I tell you."

Cinderella dried her eyes and smiled at her godmother.

"First, I want you to go into the garden and bring me the biggest pumpkin you can find," said the fairy godmother.

"Very well," said Cinderella, as she ran off to the garden. She picked the biggest pumpkin she could find and took it to her fairy godmother.

The fairy godmother touched the pumpkin with her magic wand. Immediately it turned into the most wonderful carriage you can imagine. The outside was made of shining gold and the inside was lined with red velvet.

"Now run and fetch me the mouse-trap from the pantry," said the fairy godmother.

"Very well," replied Cinderella, as she ran off to the pantry. She found the mouse-trap on the floor, behind the pantry door. There were six mice in it.

Cinderella brought the mouse-trap to her godmother. One touch of the magic wand and the door of the mouse-trap flew open. Out ran the six mice, one after the other.

As each mouse was touched by the magic wand, it changed into a fine grey horse. Six fine grey horses, to pull the golden carriage!

"Next, run and fetch me the rat-trap from the cellar," said the fairy godmother.

"Very well," said Cinderella, as she ran down the steps to the cellar. She found the rat-trap, with one rat in it, and took it to her god-mother.

One touch of the fairy wand and the rat-trap flew open and out ran the rat. The fairy godmother touched the rat with her wand and it changed into a smart coachman, dressed in red livery, trimmed with gold braid.

"Lastly," said Cinderella's godmother, "I want you to run and bring me the two lizards that are behind the cucumber frame, at the bottom of the garden."

"Very well," said Cinderella, as she ran into the garden. She looked behind the cucumber frame and there she found two small lizards, which she brought to her godmother.

Cinderella's fairy godmother touched the lizards with her fairy wand. They turned into two smart footmen, each dressed in red livery, trimmed with gold braid, to match the coachman's livery.

When Cinderella arrived at the palace, she looked so beautiful that the ugly sisters did not know her. They thought she must be a princess from another country. They never thought of Cinderella, for they believed that she was sitting at home, by the cinders.

The prince thought that he had never seen such a beautiful princess. He came towards Cinderella, took her hand and danced with her. All evening he would dance with no other maiden, and he never let her out of his sight. If anyone else came to invite her to dance, the prince said, "This is my partner."

Cinderella had never spent such a wonderful evening in her whole life. Yet she still remembered her godmother's warning.

At a quarter to twelve she left the ballroom, while the other guests were still dancing. Her carriage was waiting for her and she was driven quickly home. She arrived at the door just as the clock was striking twelve.

On the last stroke of midnight, the coach became a pumpkin, the horses mice, the coachman a rat and the footmen lizards. Cinderella's ball-gown vanished and she found herself once more in her old grey dress and wooden shoes.

Cinderella sat down in the chimney corner to wait for her sisters. When they arrived home they found Cinderella, in her dirty clothes, among the ashes and a dim little oil-lamp was burning on the mantelpiece.

The ugly sisters could talk about nothing but the beautiful princess, who had looked far lovelier than any lady at the ball. They described her gown and her slippers. They spoke of how the prince had danced with her all evening and how he would permit no other man to dance with her. Yet no one knew who she was.

Cinderella listened to all this but she said nothing.

On the next evening the ugly sisters went off to the second ball, leaving Cinderella sitting by the fire.

No sooner had they gone than Cinderella's godmother appeared again. Just as before, her magic wand produced the golden carriage with its coachman and footmen.

This time Cinderella's ball-gown was even more beautiful than on the first evening. It was made of pale blue satin, with floating overskirts of pale blue net, embroidered with silver thread. Her pale blue slippers were embroidered in silver, and silver stars sparkled in her hair.

Once more Cinderella thanked her godmother, who reminded her to be home by midnight.

When Cinderella arrived at the ball, in the blue dress, everyone was astonished at her beauty. The king's son had waited until she came and he instantly took her by the hand and danced with no one else but her. When others came and invited her to dance, he said, "This is my partner."

Cinderella was so happy that she almost forgot what her godmother had told her. When at last she did remember to look at the clock, it was five minutes to twelve. She left the prince and hurried out of the ballroom as quickly as she could.

Cinderella's carriage was waiting for her and they set off at speed. But they were only half way home when the clock began to strike twelve.

On the last stroke of midnight, the carriage and horses, the coachman and footmen vanished. Cinderella found herself, in her old grey dress and wooden shoes, in the middle of a dark, lonely road.

She had to run the rest of the way home, as fast as she could. Even so, she had just seated herself on her stool by the cinders, when her sisters returned from the ball.

Once more, all the ugly sisters could talk about was the beautiful stranger with whom the prince had danced.

On the evening of the third ball, Cinderella's fairy godmother appeared as soon as the ugly sisters had left.

When her godmother had touched her with the magic wand, Cinderella found herself in a gown which was more splendid and magnificent than any she had yet had. It was made of silver and gold lace, which shimmered as she moved. On her feet were golden slippers. Diamonds sparkled at her throat and her golden hair was held high by a dazzling diamond tiara.

Cinderella was so delighted that she hardly knew how to thank her godmother.

"Enjoy yourself, my dear," said her godmother, "but do not forget the time."

When Cinderella arrived at the ball, in her dress of silver and gold, she looked so magnificent that no one knew how to speak for astonishment.

The prince danced with no-one but Cinderella all evening and, if anyone invited her to dance, he said, "This is my partner." Cinderella was so happy that she forgot all about the time.

Suddenly the clock began to strike twelve. Cinderella was terrified that she would find herself in the ballroom in her old grey dress. She rushed out of the door in such haste that she lost her left slipper.

The prince ran after her and saw the slipper. He picked it up, and it was small and dainty and all golden.

Each of the ugly sisters was determined to squeeze her foot into the tiny slipper, so that she could marry the prince. But they both had large, ugly feet. Even though they struggled until their feet were bleeding, neither one could force her foot into the slipper.

At last, the prince turned to Cinderella's father and asked, "Have you no other daughter?"

"I have one more," replied the father, "but she is always in the kitchen." Then the ugly sisters cried out, "She is much too dirty, she cannot show herself."

But the prince insisted and so Cinderella was sent for.

Cinderella first washed her hands and face clean and then went and bowed down before the prince, who gave her the golden shoe. She seated herself on her stool, drew her foot out of the heavy wooden shoe, and put it into the slipper, which fitted like a glove.

When Cinderella stood up and the prince looked at her face, he knew it was the beautiful maiden who had danced with him. He cried out, "This is the true bride."

At that moment, Cinderella's fairy godmother appeared and turned her once more into the beautiful princess. The old grey dress became a velvet gown.

The prince lifted Cinderella on to his horse and rode away with her.

The two ugly sisters were horrified to discover that Cinderella was the beautiful princess who had been at the three balls. They were so angry that they were pale with rage.

At the palace, the King was glad to welcome his son's bride. He arranged a magnificent wedding for the prince and Cinderella. All the kings and queens, the princes and princesses, in the land, came to the wedding. The wedding feast lasted a whole week.

And so Cinderella and the prince lived happily ever after.

Series 606D

Cinderella's face was shining with joy. "Oh! thank you, godmother!" she cried, "thank you!"

"Enjoy yourself at the ball, my dear," said her godmother. "But there is one thing you must remember. You must be home before the clock strikes midnight. For, on the last stroke of twelve, the coach will become a pumpkin again, the horses mice, the coach-man a rat, the footmen lizards, and you your-self the ragged girl you were."

"I will remember," said Cinderella, as her godmother kissed her good-bye.

The footman opened the door of the car-riage. Cinderella sat down and spread out her skirts on the red velvet cushions. The coach-man touched the horses with his whip, and they were off to the ball.